The Wombat King

Other books in the After Dark series

The Wombat King

Philip Neilsen

Mark Wilson

Lothian
B O O K S

After Dark series editor
Gary Crew

Thomas C. Lothian Pty Ltd
11 Munro Street, Port Melbourne, Victoria 3207

First published 1997

National Library of Australia
Cataloguing-in-publication data:

Neilsen, Philip, 1949.
  The wombat king.

  ISBN 0 85091 792 1.

  I.Title. (Series: After dark; 13)

A823.3

Illustration media: pen and ink
Cover design by Dennis Ogden
Printed by PT, Pac-Rim Kwartanusa Printing,
Indonesia

It was morning again. Christopher yawned a slow, stretching yawn. Through the long night, while he tossed and turned under his doona, the bush outside had been alive with the scuttling and scampering of animals. A million dramas had taken place under leaf and moon, and now the participants would be returning to their burrows.

Christopher stared at the wall opposite his bed. He had covered it with photographs and drawings of wombats. His father had been angry about the drawing-pin holes in the wall, but the pictures stayed. This early in the morning, with his curtains drawn, the shapes of the animals were unclear, but that made them all the more mysterious.

He yawned again; at last he felt ready to slip into a deep, dream-filled sleep. But he heard the sounds of breakfast coming from the kitchen; his mother clattering a saucepan in the sink to warn him his time was up, that he had another school day to endure.

He dressed slowly and went down the stairs. In the kitchen his parents were standing in front of the fridge, reading a message stuck there with a magnet.

'What's this?' his father demanded. He took it down and read it aloud:

BE SILENT, BE PATIENT, BE EVERYWHERE

'Another wise saying from your nocturnal friend, I suppose,' he added sarcastically. 'How

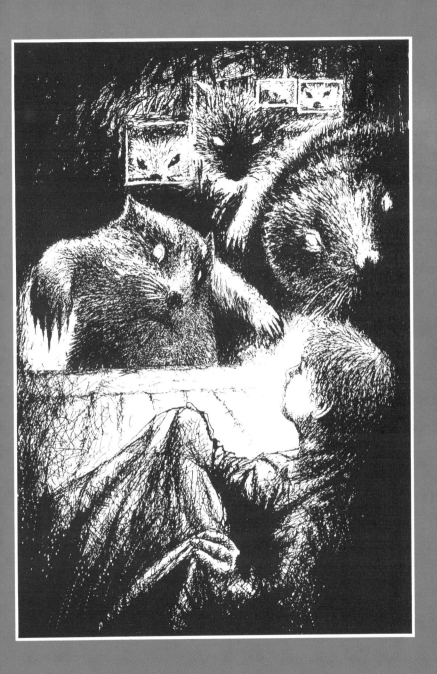

many more of these are we going to see?' He folded the piece of paper and handed it to Christopher. 'Just what are you trying to prove with this nonsense?'

'The Wombat King is always wise,' Christopher replied.

His mother knelt and peered at him. 'You look tired,' she said in a worried tone. 'Have you been lying awake all night again?'

Christopher did not answer and his father snorted angrily. 'We should never have given him those stupid stuffed toys. He still sleeps with them like a pathetic baby!' He picked up his leather briefcase and left the room. Mr Morrow designed high-rise buildings where swarms of people worked.

'Would you be happier if you had a brother or sister to play with?' his mother asked, still looking at him closely.

'I don't think so,' he said, turning to gaze out at the bush beyond the garden.

Christopher's family lived on the edge of town, next to a forest reserve. On the way to school, Christopher always made a detour along a narrow track that led through the edge of the forest. This morning he ventured further into the trees than usual, far enough to know there was no one else around. He stopped and breathed in the bush smells — sweet wattle blossom, musty eucalypt, damp earth in places where the sun had not penetrated. The morning was already growing hot, and the first cicadas had begun to shrill.

He had always been able to hear better than others. Even at school, when the teacher told the class to read the next page to themselves, he could catch fragments of sound drifting from the bush half a kilometre away: the cry of a bird defending its territory; the crack of a branch falling suddenly from an old tree.

Christopher sat down for a few minutes on a small log and closed his eyes. If he didn't go to school his father would find out. There was no way to avoid it.

He realised the cicadas had stopped. There was no sound at all except for the darting buzz of a bee, followed by silence. He held his breath and kept as still as possible. And then, very faintly, he heard something new. A sound like a heavy but careful animal walking on dead leaves. His heart beating, Christopher stared at the green and brown tangle of undergrowth where the sound had come from. He saw nothing, but he felt a tingling happiness he had never felt before.

The cicadas started up again.

The school was red brick, with an iron gate at the front. His father had wanted Christopher to go to the same school he had attended. The school where he had been famous for his sporting prowess, and for coming top in every exam. Christopher was there to build his character.

This morning his teacher was a few minutes late, detained by the headmaster as they discussed some matter of discipline. Christopher sat in the back row of the class. The old wooden desks had initials carved deeply into them. Messages from students a hundred years ago. Like prisoners' voices, Christopher thought. Beside him on the wall was a map of the world. He was grateful for this piece of luck. When he was bored he could gaze at all the colours and lines that represented rivers and mountains and jungle. The world was so large, with so many places to hide where no one could ever find you. Christopher imagined canoeing up the Amazon River or trekking over the Kalahari Desert. Often, as he stared ahead at the blackboard, his teacher's voice came drifting over the gentle splash of paddles, as he eased his way through the thick vines lying in a tangle at the water's edge, or was obscured completely by the brutal whine of desert wind outside his tent during a sand storm.

But this morning he thought of his own forest, and the sound of careful feet on dry leaves. He was straining his eyes to see a shape through the leaves ...

The door banged as Mr Mansfield entered the room and began to clean the blackboard with wide, vigorous strokes.

'Take out your maths books, quickly, and turn to page thirty-three.'

Christopher found his maths book, but while the others struggled to understand fractions he turned to the back, where there were four pages that had been left blank for notes. On the first page was a list of words he had begun compiling: *darkness, elusive, secretive, invisible, stealthy, powerful, night walker, danger*. The words helped with his drawing. On the next two pages were practice sketches, and on the fourth was the masterpiece on which he had been working. The drawing was very skillfully done. There was a clearing in the middle of a forest of tall gums. At one side of the clearing was a magnificent throne made of smooth, flat stones. And on the throne squatted a large, dark grey wombat. Underneath the picture, Christopher had printed:

THE NIGHT IS OUR HOME,
THE DAY IS DANGER

This would be the message he would stick on the fridge tonight, when his parents were asleep.

Turning back the pages to the chapter the class was trying to comprehend, he tried hard to look interested in what the teacher was saying. But

the long night vigil had been too much for him. Though he battled to stay awake, his head began to droop. When Mr Mansfield turned again to the blackboard, Christopher slipped as quietly as possible under the desk, curled up and fell asleep.

Before he could reach his dreams there was a hand on his shoulder, shaking him roughly.

'Come out of there, you disgusting little animal!' Mr Mansfield shouted. He picked up Christopher's book.

'So this is what you do when you're not sleeping in class — you scribble rubbish in your textbook!' He ripped Christopher's picture out and crumpled it in his hand.

'Go to the headmaster's office. If you don't stop this nonsense I will have to write to your parents and tell them how you behave. I'm sure your father would be especially disappointed.'

Christopher stumbled out of the room in a daze. He didn't go to the headmaster's office. He ran until he came to the tall wire fence that surrounded the school yard. Walking beside it, he came to the corner farthest from the classrooms. Here the ground was softer, since fewer feet had stamped it down while playing football. Falling to his knees, Christopher took out his pocket knife and began to dig. The ground was harder than he expected, but after a while the earth began to yield.

The sun was half-way up the morning sky, beginning to burn his arms and neck. He dug and scraped, using his fingers and the knife, and the sweet smell of the fresh, dark earth greeted him. His arms and shoulders were stronger than most other boys' and his muscles served him well. Down he dug, past the thin, ghostly roots that twisted through the topsoil, into the softer clay, until the hole was big enough to lie in.

When he curled up he slept peacefully this time, his dreams of slow, drifting clouds in the moonlight. He was with the wombats. Together they left their burrows, walking without fear along familiar paths, the fresh night bringing messages they could feel and smell. In the old days there had been too many of them to count. That was when the bush covered all the world and everywhere was home. They knew how to live with fire and flood, and there was no enemy. But then the world began to shrink. Paths that had meandered under trees were now blocked by fences or lay under concrete and bitumen.

Now those who were left were all the more precious; each guarded each, keeping to the deepest forest, waiting for the day when the fences would move back and the trees spread wide again. As they walked this night they heard the call of hunting birds. The birds made a sound like school bells.

Christopher woke to the distant babble of children's voices as they hurried out of the class-rooms.

He clambered out of the hole and frantically filled in the cavity. He stamped it flat and sprinkled some yellow grass on top. Rubbing his eyes, he made his way slowly to the headmaster's office. One of the tough boys from his class saw him knock on the dark blue door and nudged his friend to look. They laughed, then ran to catch up with some of their mates.

One look at Mr Weller's face told Christopher a long lecture was coming.

'I can't tell you how disappointed I am to see you in this room again,' the headmaster began. 'Your father's name will long shine brightly in the history of this school. He was a brilliant scholar and athlete, a boy with the highest standards in all things. And you have brought disgrace to his name.'

Christopher stood numbly. He tried to imagine himself still walking under the night trees, but he could see nothing.

Mr Weller's voice filled the small room. Christopher heard the usual phrases: 'privilege of an excellent education ... obligation to parents ... laziness will not be tolerated ...'

The headmaster stopped and Christopher mumbled, 'Yes, sir.' The man was looking with disgust at the dirt stains on Christopher's knees and hands.

'You will go home now. And you will not return to school until you are willing to maintain the school's standards of cleanliness. This is your last chance.'

Christopher left the office and quickly walked to the end of the verandah and down the stairs. Under the building were some taps. He splashed water on his knees and did his best to wash the dirt off. He could see nothing wrong with dirt, could not understand why people were so afraid of it, but he preferred to avoid a second lecture about hygiene from his parents.

It was quite a long walk home. He plodded on, barely noticing where he was going. The gardens of the houses he passed were all much the same — neat little flower beds and concrete driveways. The white picket fences were too flimsy to resist a wom bat's strength. How they would laugh at them. And what use were these gardens? The lawns were short and leafless with mowing and raking, the well-clipped shrubs threw only a thin shade. There was nowhere an animal could rest in the heat of the day or be safe from prying eyes.

As he turned a corner something hard smashed into his chest. He was lying on his back, unable to breathe. Above was the sky and the red flowers of a flame tree and then the face of the boy who had seen him outside the headmaster's office. The boy had a backpack full of books in his hand.

'Down on the ground where you belong, eh, feral?'

There was laughing. Then his arms were grabbed and two other boys were kneeling on them. He still couldn't breathe properly.

'We didn't see you at lunchtime, feral. We're really worried you missed your lunch. Lucky for you we've got some of your favourite food.'

More laughter and giggling. Hands were pressing leaves and soil into his mouth, trying to make him eat it. They rubbed the stuff all over his face. He started to choke and cough. Then they were gone.

He sat up and spat out the mess in his mouth. There were bits of red in it from the flame tree. He knew its leaves were poisonous.

He looked around him carefully. There was no sign of them, but they could be waiting for him at the bottom of the hill. The fences were higher there and no one would see. He turned back and walked quickly down another street, every now and then glancing over his shoulder.

Three more blocks and still he was OK. There was a short cut across some land that had been cleared of trees for a new housing estate. The mangled earth was furrowed and criss-crossed by the huge wheels of heavy machines. Now a single yellow bulldozer stood on its own.

At the edge of the estate there was a stack of long concrete pipes. Christopher crawled into the middle of one. It was cool and dark. He rubbed his arms and felt his swollen mouth. He lay down and drank in the quiet. At the end of the pipe he could see a circle of light that looked like a shining globe of the world. It was comforting to have it there if he wanted it. Like the map beside his desk at school, it showed that the whole world could be squeezed into a small space.

After a while he could hear soft sounds and whispers, as if reaching up to him from the earth. Telling him everything was all right:

THE TRUE WORLD LIES BELOW

The next day there was sports practice after school. Christopher lugged the new football boots his father had given him down to the changing sheds. He ran his hand over the hard plastic studs that jutted from the soles of the boots. Following the other boys, he clattered his way along the concrete path to the oval. Why can't we run in bare feet? he thought.

As the sportsmaster divided them into two teams, Christopher hung back behind the others. Eventually he was sent to the edge of the field. He smelled the newly mown grass and hoped the ball would not come his way. He tried scuffing at the ground with his heavy boots. The studs bit into the earth and he began to scrape away at the surface with them. There was sudden confusion and shouting, and he looked up to see the ball wobbling and bouncing towards him. He knew he was supposed to stop it. As it slithered nearer he ran forward and fell on it, clutching it to his chest. Two boys sprang on top of him, then several others joined in, their rough hands trying to wrench the ball away from him. He rolled himself into as small a shape as he could, but a fist numbed his ear and a knee found his ribs. He could not breathe. Then an ugly voice spat: 'Kill the feral! Don't let him go!'

He forgot the ball and kicked and pushed back at them. They were surprised at his strength. Others took up the chant: 'Get the feral!' A hand closed around his throat. He managed to pull the hand away and sink his teeth into it.

In a matter of seconds, the boys had rolled off him and he felt the cool air again. The sportsmaster was standing over him, shrilling his whistle with a flushed face. Christopher leapt to his feet and ran. He crossed the field, past a group of girls playing netball, and kept running until he reached the back fence of the school.

When the sportsmaster found him he was sitting cross-legged on top of a rubbish bin. He was panting, his eyes closed.

'What do you think you're doing there, boy?' the master demanded. He banged three times on the side of the bin. It made a deep, hollow sound.

'Come on, lad, don't play the fool. Those boys were rough with you, but you weren't joining in the game properly. You have to try to fit in more. Do you hear me?'

Christopher heard only the rasping sound of a crow complaining from its branch; the late afternoon wind made its soft roar in the treetops; a goanna's claws scuttled up an ironbark's tough hide.

The master walked away.

The Wombat King was on his throne. He did not answer to anyone.

That night Christopher lay in bed, waiting. When he was certain that his parents were fast asleep, he put on his tracksuit and took a black knapsack from under his bed. It contained a torch and mosquito repellant. He slid the bedroom window open very carefully, climbed over the sill and dropped to the lawn.

For the next two weeks he spent almost every night in the forest, returning to his room at dawn. He took care to brush any leaves and twigs from his tracksuit before folding it and placing it in his drawer. He had not seen the wombats yet, but he knew they were there.

One pale morning, as he was climbing wearily back in the window, he overbalanced and fell heavily. His father rushed in to find him sprawled on the carpet. There were dry leaves in his hair and grass seeds clinging to his legs.

'So — it's come to this!' his father said coldly, hands on hips, standing there in his neat pyjamas. 'We've trusted you. We've given you the best education, a safe roof over your head, and you betray our trust.'

Christopher lay there, unable to speak. He could see the veins bulging on his father's neck.

'You spend the night crawling around in the bush like a wild animal. You do it to spite your mother and me. Well, this has been the last time.' He left the room without another word.

When Christopher came home from school that afternoon, he found that his father had hammered nails into his bedroom window so that it could not be opened. Christopher looked out towards the edge of the bush. The low sun on the glass made the trees seem far away.

'I have to get out,' he said to himself. 'I must. They will be expecting me.'

Later, after he had said goodnight to his mother, he took his doona and pillows and arranged them under the bed to make a soft cave. He squirmed into the tight space and lay there, gazing up at the window. The hours passed but he did not sleep.

The next morning his father read a new note on the fridge:

NO PRISON WILL HOLD THE KING

He looked sternly at Christopher. 'The headmaster has spoken to me. He says you are a daydreamer. Immature. You fall asleep in class.' His voice hardened. 'And you bit a boy at football practice. The school will have no place for you if you can't behave like the others. I know, I went there. I knuckled down, I obeyed the rules, and I came out on top. Well, what do you have to say?'

Christopher could not meet his father's eyes. His voice was unsteady. 'The other kids shouldn't bully me.'

'No,' said his father. 'They shouldn't. And if you stop this childish wombat nonsense I'm sure they won't. It's a hard world out there. If you don't grow up quickly, it will eat you alive.'

The next day was Saturday. Christopher dressed in his tracksuit and sneakers and walked out to the back yard, where his parents lounged, reading the papers by the pool. He noticed a single gum leaf floating in the chemical-clean water.

He stood next to his father. 'The Wombat King wishes to see you,' he said in a confident voice. His father ignored him and kept reading.

Christopher took a deep breath. 'He desires your presence,' he repeated more loudly.

The pool pump sucked at the cold blue water with a deep droning.

His mother turned to them. 'Why don't you two boys camp out in the forest tonight?' she said. 'It will be good for you to have some time together.

We haven't used that tent once since we bought it.'

Mr Morrow pulled a face, but got up slowly and walked to the house.

Not long after, with Christopher leading the way, father and son squeezed under the post-and-rail fence and were enveloped in the warm, humming forest. They followed a faint path between the acacias and tall stringybarks. Mr Morrow, carrying the heavy pack on his back, stopped now and then to pull the sticky green grass seeds from his clean white running socks.

They walked through bracken and small blue flowers, sometimes descending into gullies or stepping over fallen trees. Christopher turned off the path into thicker bush. Now and then he checked his father's face, but saw no sign of annoyance. Mr Morrow was holding a small branch in front of him to clear the spider's webs. A sleek mobile phone was hooked on the elastic waist of his shorts.

'When I went bushwalking as a boy, we used to sing songs,' he announced in a deliberately cheerful voice. 'I'll teach you some.'

He began singing a hearty hiking song. The

bush seemed to grow quieter in response, recoiling from the strange sound. Christopher wondered how to make him stop. Then the mobile phone shrilled. Mr Morrow pressed the black object to his ear. They kept on walking.

Whatever the call was about, it made Mr Morrow angry.

'Don't argue with me — I told you I wanted the foundations finished by Monday,' he shouted into the phone. 'If you can't do it, I'll hire someone else.'

Preoccupied with his call, Mr Morrow didn't notice the rocks hidden by the grass. He tripped and fell, the phone flying from his hand. As his father got to his feet, Christopher retrieved the phone. The clear plastic face was smashed. His father snatched it from him, stabbing anxiously at the buttons. He pressed it to his ear, but it said nothing to him. He shoved it into his backpack and glared at his son.

Christopher began walking again and his father followed.

It was late afternoon. Across the ridges the sun cast a luminescence on the pale bark of the gums and on the dark leaves of the scrub. As they went deeper into the forest, the trees became taller and straighter and there was less space to walk between them. They saw fewer birds in the branches above them. There were small plants with red and green leaves clustered here and there, some with soft yellow spikes protruding from their centres. Mr Morrow stopped and puzzled over them.

'I've never seen anything like this before. These trees are much older than I would have expected so close to the estate. There shouldn't be so many treeferns in this climate either. And how does this grass grow with so little sunlight? It doesn't make sense.'

The air had suddenly become cooler. They moved on, more slowly, the man now silent. Christopher felt a lightness start to flow to his heart.

The forest was now so dense that Mr Morrow almost had to squeeze between the trees. Then Christopher stopped. In front of them was a clearing. There was little to see but fine tufts of grass and some young wattles. Here and there, just visible through the grass, were holes in the ground. They were about a metre wide and almost as deep, and around their edges were rows of small rocks. When they stood in the clearing and their eyes grew accustomed to the light, Mr Morrow noticed that at the far edge of this space stood some poles that had been cut from saplings and were now grey with age. They had been braced by other poles to make rough triangles. There was a strange feeling about the place.

Christopher sat cross-legged. 'This is the Lost City of the Wombat King,' he whispered.

His father looked about, then sat beside him, chuckling. 'I can see why you might think that,' he said, 'but these are the remains of a gold-mining camp from last century. People flocked to any place that had some gold then. Those holes are mineshafts that have gradually been filled in. Those poles are what is left of the frames for their buildings.'

'No.' Christopher shook his head firmly. 'This is the Lost City of the Wombat King. We must wait for him.'

'It's good to have an imagination, Christopher,' Mr Morrow softened his voice. 'But you know very well that wombats disappeared from around here years ago. People needed the land for houses.' He paused. 'Humans need somewhere to live too.'

'The wombats were here first,' Christopher replied. 'And now they're back.'

His father started to argue, but Christopher put his finger to his lips, and Mr Morrow said no more.

They sat there until it was nearly dark. Christopher did not move, but his father shifted his weight every few minutes. He reached out to pick up twigs, or crushed leaves between his fingers to smell the sap. Nothing came except a crow, which flapped awkwardly down to a branch close by and called twice with its ugly cry. Mr Morrow threw a stick at it and it flew away.

In the last light they put up the small blue tent and spread their sleeping bags inside. They ate some sandwiches as the night sounds closed around them. Christopher's father told him how he had always been afraid of the bush at night when he was a boy.

'Afraid of the bush?' Christopher found this very strange.

'Oh, yes,' Mr Morrow laughed, 'I thought it was full of horrible monsters. So *my* father made me join the scouts — and soon I became a scout leader. I lost my fear — going on long hikes, singing songs together round the camp fire.'

'But you never spent the night alone in the bush,' said Christopher.

His father was silent for a while. 'The important thing, Christopher, is that I learnt how to get along with others. And I realised that I had been silly when I was younger — silly to let my imagination invent monsters — to make up things that weren't real.'

'The Wombat King isn't a monster.'

His father sighed and turned over to sleep.

Christopher lay awake as he always did, listening to the bush talk. Sometimes there was a rustle, or a beating of wings, or a high-pitched squeal, but he did not hear any slow footsteps on dry leaves.

Perhaps he dozed for a few minutes. He became aware of the moon casting the weird shadow of a tree on the side of the tent. Then his heart stopped. Another shape appeared on the thin nylon. An indistinct, but familiar, rounded shape. He was sure he could just see an ear and a nose. The shape moved slightly, as if hoping to be seen.

He shook his father awake. 'Dad, look!' he whispered. 'Look — he's outside!'

Mr Morrow glanced at the side of the tent with half-closed eyes and rolled over again. 'Don't be silly. It's just the shadow of a wattle or something. There's nothing out there — go back to sleep.'

Christopher looked again, but the shape was gone. He stared at the place where it had been for a long time. He did not sleep again.

At dawn they packed up the tent and slowly walked back home. The dew soaked into their socks. Mr Morrow groaned and said that sleeping on the hard ground had ruined his back. He took out his mobile phone and jabbed at its useless buttons. That put him in a worse temper.

Neither of them spoke again.

The next day Christopher's mother glanced into his room and saw that he had taken down all his wombat pictures and gathered the stuffed toys — the two wombats and the platypus — and put them in a carton. The doona and pillows were back on his bed, neatly arranged. And there was a message, in bigger letters than ever, on the fridge:

THERE CAN ONLY BE ONE LEADER

She told Christopher's father about the photos and toys and the new message. 'He means me,' Mr Morrow replied with satisfaction. 'At last he's coming to his senses.' He put his arm around his wife's shoulders. 'That awful night in the bush wasn't wasted. I told him about my own experiences as a boy — how I had to become tough. It must have sunk in.'

He found his hammer and pulled the nails out of Christopher's bedroom window. 'I think we should show we trust him now,' he said. He gave his wife a kiss on the forehead.

That night Christopher went to bed immediately his parents told him to. He closed his eyes and, when his mother came to the door, pretended to be asleep. The moonlight began to move across the blank wall where the pictures had been. Christopher waited and listened. It took a long time, but then he heard it, more clearly than ever. The rustling of the grass, the slow, soft sound of careful feet on dry leaves. They were just outside the window. He quietly got out of bed and took his tracksuit from the drawer.

In the morning, there was a new message on the fridge:

TOGETHER WE WILL
FIND A HOME